Amish Christmas Hope

©2018 by Ka

This is a work of fiction. Names, characters, places and incidents are a product of the author's imagination. Any

Chapter One

Mary King blinked her eyes open, taking in the sun shining through the bedroom window. It seemed the earth was awake early that morning and, even from her place in the bed, she could hear the birds already at play on the branches of the tree nearby. Even though it was December, the morning already seemed unusually warm and bright.

What day was it?

Mary didn't even have to ask herself – as soon as she awoke, the upcoming events of the day were the first thing that came to mind.

This was the day of the wedding.

Smiling to herself, Rachel considered how the dawn of a new day meant something joyful for the Kalona Amish community – this day was the start of a new life for Mary's best friend, Willa.

Turning on her side, Mary looked at her friend who was sleeping on the other side of the mattress. Mary had chosen to spend the previous day, and the night, with Willa, giving them the opportunity to put touches on last-minute wedding details.

While several of their young, unmarried female friends had stayed to help, Mary had been the one who had gone to sleep last, and the one who awoke first. Stretching her arms above her head, she smiled to herself before reaching out to give her friend a nudge.

"Wake up, Willa!" she called out in a sing-song voice, "Wake up, sleepy head!"

Looking around the room, Mary watched as some of the other young women began to yawn and blink their eyes, obviously surprised to see the rays of sun already illuminating the bedroom.

Willa's eyes were the last to flicker open, a confused smile on her face as she looked around the room.

Giggling to herself when she looked at her friend's surprise, Mary asked, "Do you know what day it is?"

Slowly, Willa began to nod her head as realization hit her conscious mind, "Yes," she whispered, "I'm getting married today!"

As reality hit all the young women, they quickly became alert and excited. Jumping to their feet, they practically scurried around the bride-to-be and began to sing. Giggles reigned supreme as several of the girls made comments about the upcoming wedding.

"*Ach*," Lizzie Stoltzfus exclaimed as she held her hands to her cheeks, "To think that dear Willa will soon be a bride!"

"And....soon after, a *Mamm*!" Ada Miller added, throwing her body across the bed and almost squashing Willa in the process.

The group of girls giggled, and Mary watched as Willa's face turned bright red.

"Now, now, girls," Willa scolded, her embarrassment so great that it seemed difficult for her to even speak, "Let's not go talking about babies any time soon."

Her comment sent a new round of laughter around the room, and Ada added, "Seeing the way that Carl looks at you, I'd say it won't be long before you have a whole house of children!"

Watching her friend, Mary soaked in the joy that Willa was experiencing. Willa was a good girl, and Mary could not be happier to see her get married.

"Hush, you sillies!" Mary exclaimed, "She's got to get dressed or she'll be missing her own wedding!"

Since their plain community didn't practice the wedding rituals of the modern Englisch world, Willa dressed in a simple but fresh new blue dress. Her blonde hair was brushed back into the usual bun and hidden beneath her prayer *kapp*.

Despite the plain clothing, Willa still looked like a picture. Standing on the sidelines, Mary found herself staring at her friend, overwhelmed by how beautiful the young bride truly was. Taking the moment to glance at the grandfather clock on the nearby wall, Mary gasped when she realized the time. Giving her friend a quick hug, she rushed to get ready herself.

As she pulled on her own fresh, blue dress, she considered how quickly time was changing things within their community.

Everything was changing…except for Mary herself.

At eighteen-years-old, Mary King was a pretty enough girl, she supposed, although she generally considered herself to be average. She was about regular size for her age with a slim body. On her cheek, Mary had a single dimple that gained her plenty of teasing from her friends; despite the teasing she received, she always appreciated the dimple…her parents had always called it the touch of *Gott*. That alone gave her a sense of pride.

Glancing across the room at Willa, Mary made the final touches on her own hair before placing her prayer *kapp* on her head. She and Willa had been friends for as long as she could remember, and Mary knew that they would always be friends. She was so happy that Willa had found true love; however, deep in her heart, she had to admit that she was somewhat jealous. While all of her other friends were finding beaus and husbands, it seemed that Mary was destined to stay single for the rest of her life.

Making her way across the room, she took the opportunity to give Willa her good wishes before they became busy with the wedding ceremony.

"You look so gorgeous," she told Willa, touching her cheek as she walked past her friend.

"You are not looking too bad yourself," Willa commented, her face practically glowing with joy.

"Well, I could only try," Mary laughed, looking lovingly at her friend and forcing the feelings of jealousy out of her heart.

"It's time," the voice of Willa's mother spoke from outside the bedroom door.

"Are you ready?" Mary asked her as she took one of her friend's hands in her own.

Willa took a shaky breath and nodded her head, "*Jah*, as ready as I guess I'll ever be!" With that, she turned and started out the door…toward her future with her new husband. Mary and the other ladies followed her in accordance.

The wedding party gathered out in the barn where the entire Amish community had come together to watch Willa be joined together with her new husband.

Sitting down beside her mother on one of the hard, wooden church benches that had been placed in the barn, Mary watched as the minister started the long ceremony. She had to battle tears of joy as the familiar ritual took place that signified Willa becoming one with her fiancé Carl.

When the wedding ended, Mary followed the crowd to the home of Willa's parents where they had tables lined with plates and delicious food. While most Amish receptions were held outdoors, the chilly December wedding made that impossible. Watching Willa and Carl take their places at the head of the main table, Mary felt a jolt of loneliness stab her heart. The couple fit together so well – even now, it was easy to see that they were made for each other.

Rather than dwell on her own problems, Mary allowed herself to enjoy the chance to visit with her family and friends. Gathering with some of her old childhood girlfriends, she let herself laugh with them as they recounted all of their weddings. At each wedding, they had made promises that nothing would change, that they would still remain just as close…but that had been far from reality. While they still saw each other often, it was never the same. Her friends' priorities had shifted from having fun to taking care of their husbands and the babies that they started to welcome into the world.

Glancing across the group of Amish, Mary looked at Willa once again. While it was a riot to laugh over the promises that her other married friends had broken, it made her question her future friendship with Willa. Willa was the last of her close friends to get married and now…well, now she was probably going to forget about Mary and instead focus solely on her new family.

Swallowing hard, Mary considered how quickly life changed. For a long time, Willa had been so shy around men – that was until Carl came into her life.

Willa caught her eye, and Mary watched Willa give her a happy smile. Mary found herself praying that the two of them would remain close, although her heart was telling her differently.

"Are you ready to go?" Mary's mother asked as she walked past her, reaching out to put a hand on her shoulder, "Your *Daed* says that it's about time."

Mary nodded her head slowly. As she followed her parents toward their waiting buggy, she saw that the sun was already becoming covered with dark clouds. Thankfully, the rain had held off until the ceremony was over. Something about the overcast day seemed to mirror Mary's own feelings. She knew that things with Willa would never again be the same. Losing a best friend was never easy…and just because she knew that Willa would be happy didn't dull the aching in her own heart.

Chapter Two

"Mary?"

Mary had been so tired that she had fallen asleep immediately after returning home from the wedding. All of her planning and preparation for her friend's big day had obviously taken a lot out of her...more than she had expected or realized.

"Mary," the gentle voice repeated. Sitting up, Mary squinted her eyes in the early morning light. She looked to her mother who was standing in the doorway before glancing at the wind-up clock that sat beside her bed.

It was already six-thirty in the morning! She had overslept.

"Oh my goodness!" Mary exclaimed as she threw her feet over the side of the bed and looked up to meet her mother's gaze, "I slept in. I am so sorry!"

"It's fine," Mrs. King assured her with a good-natured smile, "Your *Daed* and I decided that it was only right for you to get some rest after your big day yesterday. You worked hard, and it was easy to see that you were worn out. But now the chores are almost finished and breakfast is on the table…it's time for you to come downstairs to talk."

Before Mary could even start to wonder aloud what they might need to talk about, her mother stepped back into the hall, closing the bedroom door behind her.

Pulling herself to her feet, Mary plodded across the chilly hardwood floor and pulled a plain green dress out of her closet.

Jerking it over her head, she worked to rearrange her hair before hiding it beneath her Amish prayer *kapp*.

"Good morning, *Daed,*" she greeted as she wandered into the kitchen downstairs. Her father was seated at the breakfast table with a newspaper spread out in front of him while Mary's mom hurried to get the morning meal finished.

As they exchanged pleasantries, Mary felt her heart beat faster. Her mother had said that they needed to talk to her…what on earth about? Could she have done something wrong?

"Sit, Mary," Mr. King announced as he motioned toward her chair and closed his paper.

Tentatively taking a seat, Mary waited for the worst.

"Your *schweschder* – Joan," her father started slowly, "well, she gave birth to a baby boy yesterday."

Mary smiled. What wonderful news! Her older sister had gotten married over three years earlier, leaving their community for another village far from Kalona. This little boy would be her second child.

"I am so happy!" Mary exclaimed as she clapped her hands together. Not only was she happy for her sister but also that the conversation was nothing more serious. She had been so afraid that her father was going to scold her for some unknown sin that she had committed.

"They will be arriving here for Christmas in a few days' time," her mother added.

Mary felt her smile slowly turn into a frown. While her parents might be telling her happy news, it seemed that there was no joy evident on their faces. Regardless of her sister's good fortune, there was obviously something sinister beneath the surface.

"What is wrong?" Mary forced herself to ask, "Is this all that you wanted to talk to me about? Surely a new grandbaby would not put such long faces on you two."

Suddenly, the room grew quiet. Mary's mother put the last of the food on the table and sat down across from her.

"How old are you now?" Mary's father asked slowly as he reached out to spoon some fresh bacon onto his plate.

Crinkling her brow, Mary tried to understand her father's question, "You should know…I am eighteen now, *Daed*."

Taking in a deep breath, her father continued, "Then you should know that you are of age."

"Of age?" she repeated. Mary thought she knew what her parents were getting at but wanted to make sure before she commented.

"Yes, of age," her mother told her as she motioned toward the fresh biscuits, "I was your age when I was married."

Mary caught her mother glancing across the table at her father.

As her face grew warm, Mary had to look down at her lap. She had long known that this day would come, but she hadn't expected it here so quickly. Of course, she had thought the same thing…especially since all her friends were now married, but thinking about it did no good. No matter how much she might want to be married, absolutely no boys in the Amish community liked her…at least not in that way. They all only thought of her as a friend.

"Don't you want to get married?" her mother pressed.

Gathering her courage, Mary sat up straighter in her seat and replied, "I do wish to get married and have a family of my own…one day."

"Then why no beau?" her father pressed somewhat impatiently.

"There is nothing I can do about that, *Daed*," Mary returned, her defenses starting to rise, "No one has asked for my hand, and no one has asked for me to even go on a buggy ride with them."

Quiet ensued. Mary was shocked that this matter had even been brought up. Willa's wedding certainly must have triggered her parents into taking action.

"Why have you not been asked?" Her father finally pressed, raising his voice slightly.

Mary didn't know how to reply; instead, she just wiggled in her seat.

"Mary," her mother cut in, "What your *Daed* is trying to say is that you have not been serious about it." She paused as if the conversation was difficult for her to continue. "Even though you say you want to start a family, you are not taking action toward that goal."

Mary felt almost exasperated, "I don't really understand what you mean, *Mamm*…have I been doing something wrong?"

"Mary, you are, um…playful…flirty," her mother tried to explain as she raised her hands, "Men don't take you seriously. I believe that is why they look at you only as a friend. You act the same way around every man. They don't believe they are special in your eyes. I believe they think you see them as friends, so they look at you in the same way."

"Being friendly is fine," her father took a turn speaking, "But not so flirty. You want a man to know that you like him more than the others…and in a special way."

Swallowing hard, Mary softly replied, "But there is no one I like in that way, *Daed*."

"You mean not even one eligible man in our community holds your interest?" Her father scoffed at her statement.

Mary didn't reply…she couldn't risk saying too much.

"What about Josiah or Melvin?" her mother suggested, "The last time I checked, they were not engaged…or are they?"

Taking in a deep breath, Mary shook her head, "No. They are single."

"Good!" her father exclaimed as if that solved the world's problems, "Then talk to one of them at the next singing!"

Mary simply nodded her head and forced herself to stomach some of the breakfast in front of her, glad to have the unpleasant conversation finished.

She had never been more humiliated in her life. How could her parents have said such things to her? The idea of her being flirty…well, it was absolutely ludicrous! Mary could count the times that she'd even spoken to a boy. No, her parents were obviously grasping at straws, trying their best to create a reason that their remaining daughter was not yet wed.

Biting down on a piece of bacon, Mary choked back tears.

No, she wasn't flirty…she didn't have time to flirt.

Mary only had eyes for one man, and that man was Samuel Wittmer. No other man could come close to Samuel, at least in Mary's heart. With his broad shoulders and blonde hair, he was one of the most handsome men that Mary had ever seen. But seeing him was all that she'd ever done. Since Samuel moved to their community two years earlier, he and Mary had not shared one single word. No, their only communication had been in her daydreams.

Samuel was the one man that Mary had been waiting on, but now it seemed that it was time for her to give up. She truly was getting older, her friends were getting married, and she should move forward with her life.

Yes, at the next singing, she would follow her father's orders and talk to either Josiah or Melvin.

Chapter Three

Going to the singings on Sunday nights always made Mary somewhat uncomfortable. When she first turned sixteen and was old enough to start attending the young peoples' events, she had been excited to go and spend time with her unmarried girlfriends; however, as more of the girls she knew got boyfriends and husbands, Mary grew to find the young folks' meetings more of a drag than anything else.

Sitting in church on one of the hard, wooden benches on Sunday morning, Mary took in a deep breath, trying to will her mind not to wander to the evening that awaited her.

Every Sunday morning, families within the Amish community would take turns hosting the church service at their home. After the service and a delightful group meal, there would be a short break before the host family let all the young folks gather in their house or barn for a community singing that evening.

The singings gave the unmarried teenagers the opportunity to socialize as they shared snacks, sang together, and played games. But despite all the fun of the singings, Mary realized that the ultimate goal of the gathering was for single girls and boys to meet each other, start courting, and get married.

And everyone is getting married, Mary thought to herself as she closed her eyes, *Everyone but me.*

The thought was sobering, for sure. She had tried not to think too much about being one of the oldest unmarried women in the community, but it was hard to ignore after her conversation with her parents.

Sitting up straighter, Mary found herself seeking Josiah and Melvin, watching for them across the large congregation of black bonnets and felt hats. She had promised her father that she would make an effort to talk to one of them and, like it or not, that was exactly what she was going to have to do.

But rather than spotting either of the two young men, Mary found her eyes traveling directly toward Samuel Wittmer. There he sat among the other men, his father at his side. Even from a distance, Mary could see the sparkle in his blue eyes as the light streaming in from the window caught them.

Such kind eyes. That was one of the things that had first drawn Mary toward him – the way that his blue eyes looked like a river of kindness, almost like they hugged whoever he looked at. But he never looked at Mary.

"Mary," the hissing voice of her mother took Mary by surprise. Giving her daughter a nudge, Mrs. King motioned her head toward the minister, alerting Mary that she had better sit up and take notice of the sermon rather than daydreaming.

***

By the time evening was closing in on the community, Mary was a jumble of nerves. The young people's singing was held just down the road from her own home, making it possible for her to make the short distance by foot. Mary was glad that she could walk, since the idea of hitching up the buggy seemed like a nuisance, and she hated having to ask her father for a ride…more now than ever.

"Hello, Mary!" A buggy clipped past Mary as she made her way down the paved country road. Looking up, Mary lifted a hand when she saw Sarah Schwartz and her brother, Henry, drive past.

At least Sarah doesn't have a boyfriend yet, Mary thought to herself as she lifted her skirt and hurried on.

Sarah was only a few months younger than Mary; however, the two girls had never been friends. Sarah had always seemed so pompous and full of herself; she appeared to almost scorn Mary as more than just a mere acquaintance. Knowing that Sarah still didn't have a boyfriend was one thing that Mary could be thankful for.

Getting closer to the singing, Mary could see that the yard was already full of buggies and teenage Amish folk.

Gathering her courage and pulling her shawl tighter against her shoulders, Mary made small talk with some of the other young folk as she walked toward the house.

Pushing the door open, Mary stepped inside the Amish home. The house, where church had been held only earlier that morning, had been transformed during the afternoon. The long hardwood benches had been removed, making room for tables of food and delicious snacks.

Some of the young folk had already gathered around the coal stove, warming their hands as they began to sing some of the favorite tunes.

"Hello, Mary!" Annie Mast called out as she walked past, rearranging her chubby baby on her hip.

Reaching out, Mary gave the baby a soft chuck on the chin. She could remember going to school with Annie when they were little girls; now, Annie had moved forward in life with a husband and a baby of her own. Rather than attending the singing herself, Annie and her husband were hosting it in their home. Although it was good to see her old school friend, Mary had to admit that watching Annie with her baby made her feel almost worse than ever. Would she ever get to have a husband and a family? Would she ever make her parents happy with her?

"What did ya think of Willa getting married?" Annie exclaimed with a smile on her face as she reached down to smooth a wrinkle out of her baby's dress,
"I never would have thought that would happen. As shy as Willa always was, it seemed like she might be an old maid!"

Mary tried to laugh, but the words cut deeper than she wanted to admit.

Reaching out, Annie put a hand on Mary's shoulder and announced, "I bet you'll be next!" Hurrying on to the snack table, Annie went to put a spoon in a bowl of blackberry pudding.

Would Mary be next? She wanted it to be true, but it seemed so unlikely!

Squaring her shoulders, Mary reminded herself of her father's words. She needed to take the bull by the horns and start talking to some men or else, she would never have an opportunity to be a wife and a mother.

Melvin walked past her, practically shoving her out of the way as he hurried to pull off his wet mittens. This was her opportunity! He was so close that Mary could reach out and touch him if she wanted to.

"Hello there, Melvin!" Mary forced herself to say, the words sounding ignorant to her own ears as they escaped her lips. She didn't sound at all relaxed; instead, her voice trembled, and her words practically caught in her throat.

Melvin smiled and raised a hand, but he hurried on to the fire to talk to some of the other young women.

Letting out an exhausted sigh, Mary stepped backwards…and right into someone!

Turning around on her heel, Mary was already saying, "I am so sorry…" Her words were cut short when she realized who she had stepped right into.

Samuel Wittmer.

Swallowing hard, Mary could feel the color rise to her cheeks. She felt like she should fall to the floor and attempt to hide under the table.

"I….I…" Mary listened in horror as her voice came out as a stutter, "I… didn't…I never..."

"It's fine," Samuel hurried to announce. Watching him carefully, Mary was relieved to see his face break out into a good-natured smile. My, was he ever handsome!

"Are you sure?" Mary asked, "I think I might have stepped on your foot…"

"My feet are pretty tough," Samuel assured her, leaning his arm against the wall behind him.

His words made Mary smile, his tone relaxing her nerves.

"You're Mary, right?"

Mary was so shocked to learn that he knew her name, she thought she might fall over. Her jaw dropped open, and she was so tongue-tied that she didn't know how to even respond.

"Mary?" He repeated.

Rather than attempt to speak, Mary just nodded her head up and down, bobbing it like one of the floaters on a fishing pole.

"Would ya like to go sit down?" Samuel asked, reaching out to offer her a hand, "I'm Samuel."

The idea that she wouldn't know who he was seemed almost laughable to Mary. Nodding her head once again, she motioned toward the table, "Looks like there's a couple empty seats over there."

"What song would you like to sing?" Leaning closer to her, Samuel practically whispered the words against her prayer *kapp*.

Giving a shrug, Mary felt her face break out into a smile as she admitted, "*Ach*, I like just about any song…but I sure hope it's a Christmas one. Maybe, Jingle Bells."

"Isn't it a little early for a Christmas song?"

Shrugging awkwardly, Mary smiled, "It's never too early for Christmas, is it? That happens to be my favorite holiday!"

She could only hope that Samuel wouldn't think she was foolish or childish for loving that special day so much. Christmas had always held a special place in Mary's heart.

Samuel grinned once again…and he looked directly into Mary's eyes. For the first time, it felt like she and he were alone rather than in a crowded room of other young people.

Mary knew that people locked eyes all the time and yet, in this instance, it felt different. He stared at her like she was someone special…he made Mary feel like she was his own girl.

"What song would you all like to sing?" The voice of Annie spoke up as the young people finished arriving and gathered around the long table.

Several hands shot up in the air, but Samuel's long arm seemed to reach the highest.

"Samuel," Annie called out his name, alerting him that he was welcome to introduce the first song name.

"Jingle Bells," Samuel boldly announced. Several of the other young folk laughed, one boy even reached out to good-naturedly give Samuel a slap on the shoulder, but he didn't seem at all phased.

"Jingle Bells?" Annie repeated as a smirk played at the corner of her lips.

"*Jah*," Samuel returned, completely unashamed, "I like the Christmas ones."

Nodding her head, Annie began to lead the song, giving the group a chance to join in and sing together.

As they sang the familiar tune, Mary was certain that it had never sounded any sweeter to her ears. Next to her, Samuel's voice rang out clear and beautiful. Mary felt like her heart was going to explode with happiness.

Chapter Four

Mary spent the entire night by Samuel's side. Although they were surrounded by other people, when Samuel looked at Mary, he could make her feel like the only girl in the room. She found her gaze almost magnetize to him. She felt like she needed to grab a hold on this time together and not let it go, no matter what.

By the time the singing came to an end, Mary felt like she was a bundle of nerves. Couples began to pair off, anxious to spend time together alone on their buggies. The boys would offer to take the girls home, allowing them to sit together on the hard benches of their horse-drawn buggies and often sharing thick blankets to keep them warm. This was the only chance for courting individuals to be by themselves to talk and get to know each other on a more personal level.

"Mary," Samuel seemed almost nervous for the first time that night as he turned toward her and smiled sheepishly, "I've had a good time with you tonight."

His words seemed almost too good to be true. Mary had enjoyed being at his side so much and yet, she had spent so much of the time worrying that he was not having any fun himself.

"Would you like me to give you a ride home in my buggy?"

Mary was already pulling herself to her feet, and his words hit her by complete surprise. She could have never dreamed that he would ask her such a thing! It seemed like the night had surely already been too good…she couldn't expect even more.

Shaking her head quickly, she hurried to say, "Oh, no, don't worry about it. I live right down the road…it would be ridiculous for you to take me back! I can just walk."

It looked like a shadow crossed Samuel's face, but he quickly nodded his head and forced his smile to return, "Well then, I'll go hitch my buggy. Have a good night."

Nodding back at him, Mary said, "Goodnight."

Hurrying to go gather her coat and get started home, it felt like she was walking on a cloud. Samuel had truly spent the night by her side…and he even admitted that he had a good time! How could life possibly be any better?

***

Climbing up into his buggy seat, Samuel prepared for the long, cold ride back to his family's home. Waving toward some of his Amish friends, Samuel led his horse down the road. Out of the corner of his eye, Samuel could see Mary trooping toward her own house. Even though the girl was wearing a coat, it was easy to see that she was chilly in the December night air.

Samuel felt his heart give a lurch in his chest.

He hated to see her walking home cold, but he didn't know what else he could do. Samuel had certainly made a fool of himself, offering her a ride in the buggy…a ride that she obviously didn't want.

"Who are you kidding?" Samuel asked aloud, his breath making wisps of smoke in the night air, "You made a fool of yourself the entire night!"

For the first time since he was a little boy, Samuel felt like he might cry.

Ever since he had arrived with his family in the Amish community of Kalona, Samuel had found his eyes secretly trailing after Mary King. There was something about Mary that simply stood out from the rest of the Amish girls. She was beautiful but in a simple sort of way. Rather than being showy or bold, she was a peaceful girl…the type that Samuel could envision coming home to after a long, hard day of work out on the farm.

Samuel had been holding his breath for months, simply praying for the courage to speak to Mary. Tonight, when she had stepped backwards on him, it had felt like the Lord was presenting him with the opportunity he had wanted for so long.

The night had seemed perfect. Sitting beside Mary, Samuel had actually convinced himself that she was enjoying herself - and that she liked being with him.

"What a joke." Samuel muttered under his breath as he reached a gloved hand up to wipe at his nose.

No, she didn't like him at all. As it turned out, she wanted to just get away from him as quickly as possible. She couldn't even handle the idea of a short, five minute buggy ride home.

Shaking his head to himself, Samuel made a silent vow that he would never again try that. No matter how much he might like Mary King, it was obvious that she didn't like him, and he was not going to force himself on a girl who didn't like him. No, from now on, he would direct his attention back toward some of the other unmarried young women in their community.

While Mary might be his first choice, it seemed that it was time for Samuel to give up on the hope of ever having a relationship with the beautiful girl.

***

Stepping into the warmth of her parents' house, Mary felt like everything was right in the world. For the first time in her life, she had actually had a good time with a young man at the singing…and the young man that she had liked for so long!

"I should have let him drive me home in his buggy," Mary muttered to herself as she pulled off her coat and hurried to stand by the stove.

But as much as Mary wanted a ride by Samuel, she was almost glad that she had said no. The night had been so perfect – being alone together might have resulted in her doing something stupid and that would have destroyed everything.

"Mary?" She could hear the voice of her mother call from the other room.

Setting her mittens aside to dry, Mary followed the voice of her mother and stepped into the sitting room where her parents were gathered around the fireplace. Her mother was darning a sock while her father read a book by the glow of a lantern.

"How was the singing?" her father asked as he set his book down on his lap.

"Fine," Mary replied, almost afraid to tell them the truth. Although she was so excited that she felt she might bust, she didn't want to get their hopes up too soon. They were so anxious for her to get married – if she was to tell them about Samuel now, things might not work out, and they would be crushed.

"Did you talk to any boys?" Her mother pressed.

Nodding her head ever so slowly, Mary tried to keep a silly smile from spreading across her face, "*Jah*. I talked to some boys. I spoke to Melvin and….well, and some others."

Her mother raised her eyebrows, and Mary's father slowly nodded his head.

"I'm going to bed," Mary continued, turning to head toward the stairs, "I think I just need some rest."

But as she made her way to her bedroom, Mary felt like sleep was the last thing on her mind.

"How can I possibly sleep now?" Mary asked as she stepped into her bedroom and reached for her nightgown.

Mary only knew one thing – she could hardly wait for the next Sunday night's singing!

Chapter Five

Mary spent the entire week counting down the days until Sunday and the weekly young people's singing. While there was only church service every other week, the Amish community kept the young people entertained by having singings every Sunday night.

This Sunday night's singing was to be held at a farm several miles away. Since it would be too far for Mary to walk, and her father was going to need the buggy, she had hired a paid *Englisch* driver to take her in his car.

When she arrived at the singing, Mary felt like her heart was going to pound right out of her chest. She could never remember being more nervous or excited! With each day that had passed, she had thought more and more about Samuel. Her mind had wandered in all kinds of directions, allowing her to daydream about the possibilities of what the night could hold. Was it possible that Mary and Samuel would be married within the next few months? Was he ready for that kind of a commitment?

Stepping into the home of Johnny Troyer, Mary's eyes traveled across the group of Amish young folk as she sought out Samuel.

"Hello there, Mary!" A voice spoke up close to her ear. Turning, Mary found herself staring straight into the eyes of Melvin.

Ugh. While Mary had never outright disliked Melvin, she couldn't say that she had ever liked him, either. He was a nice enough boy, but Mary knew from their time together in school that they had little in common. After spending time with Samuel, she had less use of him than ever before.

"Hello, Melvin," Mary returned, her eyes still searching for Samuel.

She spotted him walking into the house. Mary raised her hand to wave, her heart thumping even louder than ever.

But just as she raised her hand, Mary noticed something…Samuel had a girl by his side.

Squinting her eyes, Mary tried to make out who it was.

Sarah Schwartz.

Mary felt like her heart had stopped beating entirely as she watched the man that she loved stop to lean his arm against a doorway and chat with the girl she had disliked for so long. A surge of something she had never felt before started to rise up deep inside of her, and Mary wasn't sure if she felt more like crying or running right toward Sarah and giving her a shove.

Why was Samuel with Sarah?

Almost as if he could hear her thoughts, Samuel looked up, his eyes traveling across the crowded room. His blue eyes caught Mary's gaze, and he paused, obviously studying her from a distance.

Mary tried to smile, but it felt like it got lodged in her throat – instead, she just stared right back at him.

Then, Samuel looked away…back toward Sarah. From all appearances, it looked that Samuel and Sarah were together.

"So, Mary," Melvin's voice interrupted her thoughts, and she looked just in time to see him see-sawing his weight back and forth on his legs, "I didn't mean to be rude when you tried to talk to me at the last singing...I guess I was just not paying attention and had my mind on something else."

Mary wanted to say something, but all she could think about was Samuel. It felt like her heart was breaking right in her very chest.

"So," Melvin began again as he shoved his hands down in his pockets, "Are you and Samuel...I mean, I heard that he and Sarah Schwartz were seeing each other now, so I wasn't sure…Well, are ya free to sit with me tonight?"

The last thing that Mary wanted to do was sit with Melvin. If she was honest, she just wanted to turn around and go back home. But how could she do that now? She had no ride back to her house unless she called a driver to come pick her up…and then she would have to face explaining the entire situation to her parents.

Maybe her parents had been right all along. Perhaps Melvin was the one that she needed to spend time with rather than Samuel.

Gathering her courage, Mary said, "I enjoyed my time with Samuel last week, but we're not a couple. I would be glad to sit with you, Melvin."

Melvin smiled, and Mary forced herself to smile back.

But in all honesty, Mary was not glad to sit with Melvin. She was not glad at all. Sitting down at the table next to him, she thought that she might get sick to her stomach. She wanted to look at Samuel and keep up with what he was doing, but glancing at him was almost too painful to bear. No, it was better to ignore him completely and instead focus on spending time with the man her parents had suggested.

***

Samuel watched from across the room as Mary stood talking with Melvin. He then watched as she followed Melvin to a table and sat down next to him, seemingly making small talk.

Everything made sense to Samuel now. Obviously, Mary had never liked him at all – she was just being polite when she had spent time with him the previous week. The man that she really liked was Melvin. This reality made Samuel feel completely humiliated and like hiding somewhere.

He should have never even spoken to her the previous week! As far as he could tell, Mary had never looked his way before…he shouldn't have risked it!

Looking down at his side, Samuel tried to listen as Sarah Schwartz continued to talk. Sarah was a chatterbox for sure and certain. Since Samuel had moved to the community, Sarah had been one who was willing to step forward and be honest about her feelings. She obviously liked Samuel and was more than anxious to spend time with him.

Samuel only wished that he felt the same way about her. Rather than enjoy her, Samuel found that she tended to wear him out.

"Would you want to sit down together?" Sarah asked cheerfully as she pointed toward the table, "Looks like there are still some good seats left! We could chat more when we're sitting together."

Nodding his head, Samuel forced himself to say, "That would be good. Sure."

"There's nothing quite like a good singing," Sarah pratted on, reaching out to take Samuel by the sleeve and practically drag him across the room toward the table, "I love to sing! I especially like old bluegrass and country music. What about you?"

Christmas. Samuel wanted to say, *I like Christmas music*. But the words were stuck in his throat.

He tried not to even look at Mary and Melvin when he sat down with Sarah. Seeing Mary simply brought up too much pain. Samuel didn't think that he could stand any more emotional hurt than what he was already enduring. He had never believed in broken hearts but at this moment, he was starting to feel like they were a real thing.

Samuel knew one thing for sure – he would never again, no matter what he did, ever speak to Mary King.

Chapter Six

Mary could not remember a night that lasted any longer or was any more difficult to endure. Sitting with Melvin at her side, Mary squirmed in her seat, only wishing that the minutes would go by quicker.

When the young folks finally started leaving and the room began to clear out, Mary didn't feel like she could get up from her seat fast enough. The night had been so stressful that she felt a headache starting to come on, and the tears that she had long been holding back were threatening to overwhelm her.

"Thanks for sitting with me, Mary," Melvin announced before she could scoot her chair back against the hardwood floor.

It took all of Mary's courage to plaster a smile on her face and reply, "Thank you for asking me."

Somewhere behind her, Mary could hear the obnoxious voice of Sarah Schwartz.

"Are ya driving home by yourself, Samuel?" Sarah was asking, her voice ringing out above the rest of the young people. "I don't suppose you'd have a spare seat that you could share with me, would you?"

Turning her head ever so slightly, Mary watched as Samuel gave a nod. Then, horror of all horrors, Sarah reached out and wrapped her arm around Samuel's, allowing him to lead her out to his buggy.

Swallowing hard, Mary gritted her teeth together as she watched them disappear out the back door toward Samuel's waiting buggy.

"Would ya?" Melvin's question took Mary by complete surprise. It seemed that he had asked her something, but she hadn't been paying enough attention to know what it was.

"Would I what?" she asked absent-mindedly.

"Would you be willing to let me drive ya home in my buggy?"

His words seemed almost painful in Mary's ears. *No,* she wanted to scream, *No, I don't want to go with you! I want to go with Samuel!* But there was no point in ever admitting that. Samuel had obviously chosen Sarah over her.

Nodding her head ever so slowly, Mary made herself reply, "Jah, sure, Melvin. That would be very nice."

It wasn't at all nice, but Mary wasn't sure what she could possibly do differently. Her parents had requested that she get a boyfriend and had even suggested Melvin…now it seemed that she had the perfect opportunity to go through with their wishes. There was obviously no longer a point in waiting on Samuel since he cared more for Sarah than her. And more practical than all her other thoughts, Mary realized that she truly needed a ride home.

As Melvin's buggy rolled down the road, Mary found that conversation was growing easier with each passing minute.

"Look up there at those stars!" Melvin exclaimed as he pointed up at the sky, "On nights like this, the dark sky seems so clear, you could almost get lost looking at it."

Glancing up at the sky, Mary smiled softly before turning to look at the young man beside her.

In all honesty, Melvin was not a bad looking boy; in fact, he was actually quite handsome. And more importantly than that, he was a pleasant, respectful, gentle sort of fellow.

He's the type of man that any smart girl would want for a husband, Mary thought to herself as she grew more somber by the moment.

"You know," Melvin announced, shuffling the reigns in his hands, "I've actually wanted to ask you to take a ride with me in my buggy for quite a while now. I just…well, I guess I was just too nervous…Last week, when you spoke to me, it gave me sort of a boost of courage."

Mary felt herself sinking down in her seat, her emotions more torn and confused than ever before.

"I've been interested in a lot of girls before," Melvin admitted with a shrug, "No offense intended, but you weren't really one of them. I just guess that I'd never noticed you before…but then, when you spoke to me, well, things just sort of changed."

As he made his confession, Melvin turned to look at Mary, a bashful smile on his handsome face.

"After last week, when you sat with Samuel, I was afraid that I'd blown my chance entirely. It looked like you all were sure having fun together."

The newest comment felt like a knife stabbed right into Mary's chest. Looking down at her gloved hands, she began to knead them together as she tried to think of the right words to say.

"Well," she began slowly, "Sometimes looks can be deceiving, I suppose."

That was true enough. She had been thoroughly convinced that Samuel was having a good time with her but now, looking back, Mary realized that he had surely just been tolerating their time together. He had led her on and for that, Mary didn't think she could ever forgive him.

"I know this is just a buggy ride," Melvin started again, "But I want you to know that my parents have been on me for weeks now about getting a girlfriend."

Mary couldn't stop a chuckle from escaping her lips as she admitted, "And my parents are after me to get a boyfriend. They just can't seem to wait to have an empty house."

Melvin and she both laughed together and for a moment, Mary forgot about her worries.

"I want to make them happy," Melvin finished his thoughts as he reached out and put a hand on top of Mary's, "And no matter what happens between us, I want you to know that it just seems like a Christmas miracle that I have someone by my side."

Looking at his hand on top of hers,

Mary had to swallow hard once again. She felt like gagging and yet, at the same time, his words were so sweet that she almost felt herself softening toward him.

It was certainly time for her to throw off her childish dreams of a life with Samuel and instead, embrace reality.

***

If there was one thing that Sarah Schwartz liked to do, it was talk. Samuel realized this truth more by the minute, and he found himself wishing that their buggy ride was over.

"My goodness," Sarah was bubbling on, "I sure am glad you gave me a ride tonight. My brother usually takes me back and forth from the singings, but he has a girlfriend now…and I sure don't want to just be a third wheel."

Giving a slow nod, Samuel heard himself say, "I'm happy to take you home." As soon as the words were out of his mouth, he wished that he hadn't said them.

Sarah's eyes got wide, and she scooted even closer to him, "Oh, Samuel. You truly are a wonderful man! I appreciate that so much."

Gritting his teeth together, Samuel realized that he had just accidentally agreed to take her home every Sunday night.

Oh well. At this point, it didn't really matter. Samuel wasn't going to be happy no matter what, so he might as well do what he could to help Sarah have an easier time getting home.

Chapter Seven

Standing outside the door of the small, white Amish shed, Mary tightened her hands on the handle of the wicker basket that she held against her body. Inside the handmade basket, she had lined a white cloth napkin and filled the basket with delicious homemade sticky rolls.

Just what Willa likes best, Mary thought to herself as a smile teased her lips.

The door to the shed swung open, revealing Willa. The young woman's eyes got wide, and her lips spread into a gigantic grin when she saw Mary.

Opening the door wider, Willa exclaimed, "Mary, what a wonderful treat! I didn't expect a visit! Come on inside!"

Stepping into the small, one-room shed, Mary soaked in the warmth of the cook stove. While the shed was small and primitive, it was located on Carl's parents' farm, giving him the opportunity to live alone with his new wife while still helping out his family and working to raise money for a homestead of his own.

Studying her friend, Mary honestly admitted, "Willa, you're as pretty as a picture. Truly, I think you're more beautiful than ever."

Willa blushed and looked down at the floor. It seemed there was a sort of radiant glow about her now that she was married.

"*Ach*," Willa muttered bashfully, "I think married life is good for me. Carl…well, there's just nothing like being married to your best friend…and getting to spend every minute of the day with him. It just puts a new type of joy in a girl's heart!"

Each word that Willa spoke made Mary's own aching heart feel a little bit worse. She now realized that she would never have the opportunity to experience the joy that Willa was talking about.

"How is my best friend?" Willa asked gently as she reached out to touch Mary's shoulder, obviously noticing her dejected appearance.

"Oh, I've been worse…" Mary began to explain as she set the basket of buns down on the table before sinking into a seat, the weight of the last few weeks heavy on her heart, "But I've also been much better, too."

Willa took a seat across from her best friend before reaching in the basket to pull out one of the sticky treats. "Mary," she began as she took a bite of the bun, "We've always been best friends, and you've always shared everything with me…so what's going on?"

Leaning her head against her hand, Mary tried to put everything that had happened into words. "I think that Melvin and I…well, it looks like we're going to start courting."

"Oh, Mary, that's wonderful!" Willa exclaimed, clapping her hands together before sobering and stating, "Or…maybe not?"

"No, it is wonderful, Willa," Mary returned as she grabbed for a bun of her own, "Goodness knows that I want a family of my own…and my parents are anxious for me to get married. Mamm and Daed suggested Melvin, so I went out of my way to speak to him. And Melvin…well, he's absolutely thrilled."

Willa raised an eyebrow, "But you're not so thrilled?"

While Mary had come with the express purpose of sharing her struggles with her friend, putting them into words was much harder than she had expected. It felt like speaking what she was feeling was opening a flood gate of emotions she might not be able to handle.

"Melvin is a good man. A very good man. And I know that I should be happy but…" Swallowing hard, Mary felt like the tears were going to come rising up to her eyes, "But he's not…"

"He's not Samuel," Willa finished for her, obviously reading her friend's mind.

Reaching across the table, Willa put a hand on top of Mary's and whispered,

"What's going on? Why have ya given up on Samuel? I've known that you liked him since he moved here two years ago."

Shaking her head, Mary tried to explain the entire situation, "Oh Willa, he and I spent one Sunday night sitting together at singing. I thought that we had a great time…but the next week, he showed up and spends all his time with Sarah Schwartz. He doesn't like me at all…he likes Sarah!"

Willa frowned and shook her head slowly. "I can't imagine why he wouldn't like you, Mary."

"Oh, he doesn't!" Mary assured her, "He doesn't like me at all! And I know that I just need to grow up and accept reality…I need to make myself like Melvin and forget about Samuel…but it's all just so hard."

Willa was quiet for so long that Mary

began to wonder if her friend was completely speechless. Finally, Willa whispered, "Mary, if you don't care for Melvin, then it's a sad thing to just lead him on like this. He is a person…and a good person at that. Don't just use him as a second choice because you can't get what you really want. Being someone that another person settles with…well, that's no way to live a life at all. It's not fair to you and it's not fair to Melvin! What kind of marriage would that be?"

Listening to Willa, Mary realized that her friend had a point.

Looking down at her hands, she whispered, "Then what am I supposed to do? Give up Melvin? If I give him up, then I'll have nothing at all."

Moving to Mary's side, Willa put an arm around her shoulder and whispered,

"Pray. Just pray, Mary. Let *Gott* work in his time and give him a chance to perform a miracle this Christmas season."

Although Mary knew that Willa was right, she wasn't sure that she could give up on her budding relationship with Melvin. Like it or not, it seemed that he might be the best she could hope for…and a Christmas miracle didn't appear very likely.

***

Looking up at the afternoon sky, Samuel noticed some stray snowflakes start to make their way down to the ground. Samuel worked on a construction crew with several of the other Amish men in his community. This afternoon, they were working on building a large deck onto a wealthy *Englischer's* home.

"Ya doing alright there, Sam?"

Samuel looked over to see his Amish friend, Carl, coming toward him with a pleasant smile on his face. Ever since Carl had married his sweetheart, Willa, it seemed that he was constantly smiling. While Samuel was glad for his friend, realizing that he could never share in the same happiness made him feel awful.

"Why the long face?" Carl asked as he reached out to take a hammer from Samuel's grasp.

"Nothing," Samuel muttered as he looked down and kicked his black boot against a board on the deck.

Carl raised his eyebrows and let out a sigh, obviously about to step back and let Samuel have his privacy.

For the first time, Samuel realized how anxious he was to share the truth with someone else. Sucking in a deep breath, he announced, "I'm having woman trouble."

Carl's grin grew even wider as he returned, "Well, it seems like that's the story of all our lives. There's always something going on with a woman."

Frowning, Samuel admitted, "I've got myself in quite a fix. I've got one girl that likes me, but I don't like her. And the girl I like doesn't like me. It's just a mess…I'm so discouraged and disheartened that I feel like I should just stay home and never go to singings again!"

Smirking good-naturedly, Carl nodded his head, and admitted, "Yeah, I understand. Before I met Willa, I sure had my share of heartbreaks and I thought it was about time to just stay single forever. But just wait, Samuel…Gott's got someone planned out for you. There's going to be a special girl who makes you feel like she's your best friend in the world."

While Samuel realized that Carl was trying to be helpful, the words almost made him feel worse. Looking down at his feet, he muttered, "I think I already found someone who makes me feel like she's a best friend…when Mary and I sat together…" Realizing that he had let her name slip, Samuel felt his face start to grow red.

"Mary King?" Carl interrupted, pulling a nail out of his pocket.

"Yeah," Samuel admitted before rushing to say, "Don't mention it to her, but she's the one I like. I thought that we had something special…but then it turns out I was just tricking myself. I humiliated myself, and I feel like I pushed myself on her. I don't know how I was so blinded into thinking that she liked me…but I just tricked myself on that one."

Carl reached out to give him a friendly slap on the back as he announced, "Don't feel bad. You're gonna find a girl someday. Just hang in there."

Somehow, the words seemed so blank and empty that they did little to encourage Samuel; instead, they just made him feel worse.

Chapter Eight

With Christmas only two weeks away, Mary found herself overwhelmed with responsibilities for the holiday season. During the month of December, her mother would bake special treats to sell to the *Englischers* for their parties and celebrations. Mary spent most of her time helping her mother, and when her sister Joan arrived at the farm to spend a few weeks for Christmas, Mary stayed busy helping with her new baby and other children.

Mary had hoped that all of the activities of the holiday season would keep her so busy that she wouldn't have time to think about Melvin or Samuel or any of the mess that surrounded her love life. But despite Mary's deepest wishes, it seemed that she could think of nothing else. Distracting herself only worked for so long, and there was little that could take her mind off of her troubles.

"*Ach*, Mary," Joan called out one afternoon as she stood at the kitchen counter, helping their mom knead bread for a fresh batch of sticky buns, "Baby Abe is starting to cry…could ya get him for me? My hands are covered in dough!"

Nodding her head, Mary put aside the dishcloth that she had been using to hand dry some pans before hurrying over to the cradle where her precious nephew was started to squirm and make noises.

Hoisting him up into her arms, Mary looked down at the tiny face and smiled. Abe was a perfect baby with a beautiful round face and rose-bud lips. As she reached out to stroke the top of his head, Mary felt her heart give a jump as she considered how much she loved small children and wished for one of her own.

"Mary," Joan smiled as she arranged some of the dough into rolls and placed them in a baking pan, "You have such a way with children and babies. I have such a time getting Abe to calm down…but look…he's as good as gold for you!"

Mary smiled to herself, wishing that she could pull the little child against her and hold him tightly forever.

"He's just a good baby," she assured her sister.

Joan shook her head, "No. That's not it. You're just good with babies. I can't wait until you are married with one of your own."

The words felt like a knife right in Mary's heart.

Joan's face got a smirky grin as she asked, "I don't suppose you've got a fella yet, do you?"

"She sure does!" Their mother interrupted as she stepped into the room with a fresh bag of flour that she had just procured from the pantry, "Don't let her fool you, Joan...your little sister is certainly getting the attention of some handsome young men in our community."

Mary sucked in a deep breath, wishing that she could totally avoid talking about Melvin.

"*Ach*, sister!" Joan exclaimed, a cheerful smile on her face, "Do tell all!"

Shifting the weight of baby Abe in her arms, Mary muttered, "It's not really anything. I've just been spending some time with Melvin."

"He brought her home from the singing last Sunday night!" Mrs. King went on to explain, her face filled with pride.

"Wonderful!" Joan clapped her hands together and practically jumped up and down with excitement, "I am so happy for you, sister."

Looking from Joan to their mother, Mary considered her conversation with Willa. Willa had been the one to tell her that she needed to trust Gott and do what was best. Willa had pointed out that Mary shouldn't be in a relationship just to keep her family happy.

But as Mary looked at the happy expressions on those she loved best, she felt her heart sink. Everyone wanted her to get married, and it was obvious that things would never work out with Samuel. Melvin was the best that she could hope for, and it was time for her to stop thinking otherwise.

***

Samuel found that he had come to actually hate the singings. Ever since Mary had turned him down and had then shown her interest in Melvin, it had felt like torture to even get together with the young people. However, as much as he wished that he could skip them, his parents were determined that he should go on and keep attending.

And it seemed that Sarah Schwartz was beginning to depend on him to take her back and forth to the young peoples' gatherings.

"How did I get myself into this fix?" Samuel muttered to himself as he arrived at the singing with Sarah, once again, at his side. Samuel realized that if he didn't end things with Sarah soon, everyone would be expecting them to get married…and that was the last thing that Samuel wanted at this point in his life!

The singing was located at Eli Yoder's house this week. As the young people gathered and spent time talking together, Eli stood up with a smile and waved his hat in the air to gain their attention.

"Quiet, quiet!" Eli announced, "Before we begin the singing tonight, we've got something very important to do…we've got to draw names for our Christmas gift exchange! As you all know, Christmas is just over a week away…and we always exchange names so that the young folk can buy each other gifts. This is a very fun time…so everyone step up and put your name in this hat then we'll take turns drawing one out."

Despite the promises that it would be fun, Samuel had a hard time feeling like anything was enjoyable at this point.

"*Ach*," Sarah exclaimed as she stood at his side, a smile spread across her face, "A gift exchange! I hope that we draw one another's names!"

When the hat came around the room, Samuel reluctantly drew out a slip of paper.

Looking down at the name, he felt his heart stop in his chest.

"You know the rules!" Eli continued, "You can't tell anyone who your secret name belongs to…until the night when you exchange gifts."

Swallowing hard, Samuel read the name again, almost hoping that it would have changed.

Mary King.

There was no way that he could force himself to buy her a present and then give it to her. No, that would simply be too embarrassing and too heartbreaking.

Stepping up close to Eli, Samuel tried to explain, "I can't do this…Eli, I'm going to have to take a different name…"

Eli was shaking his head good-naturedly, "No, no, Samuel. You know it doesn't work that way! Be a good sport and just buy something for the name you got."

Letting out a deep sigh, Samuel shook his head sadly. It looked like he would be forced to buy Mary a gift. He could only hope that she would receive it more kindly than she had received his attention.

***

Mary rode alongside Melvin in his buggy, listening as he talked about the weather and the name that he had drawn in the exchange.

"Sarah Schwartz," Melvin announced with a laugh, "I never would have guessed that I'd get her." Shaking his head, Melvin continued, "I sure did used to like that girl."

Just the name alone made Mary feel sick to her stomach. Every week, she had to watch Sarah and Samuel together…and it was almost more than she could stand.

"Who did you get?" Melvin pried as he clucked his tongue to speed up the horse.

Mary had gotten the name of one of the younger Amish girls; however, she wasn't about to tell Melvin.

"That's breaking the rules," Mary informed him with a scolding laugh.

Despite her attempts at being cheerful, Mary's heart was heavy. It seemed that she spent all her time conflicted, torn between making her family happy by staying with

Melvin and tearing them apart when she broke things off before they got more serious.

Closing her eyes, she breathed out a prayer, "What do you want me to do, Lord? What do you want me to do?"

Suddenly, the truth came upon her. She was ignoring her better judgement and accepting Melvin's affection not because she wanted it, but because she was too scared to let him go. She wanted a husband and, rather than trust Gott to bring her one, she was determined to cling onto a man who was wrong for her. After she had been betrayed by Samuel, she had felt desperate to get a beau…even if it wasn't someone that she cared for.

"I trust you, Lord," Mary whispered her prayer, "I trust you, and I believe that you will take care of my future."

Turning to Melvin, Mary took in a deep breath and announced, "Melvin…we need to talk."

"Oh dear," Melvin muttered with a laugh, "This sounds serious!" As he examined Mary's face, his tone grew sober and he announced, "I think this must really be serious!"

Swallowing hard, Mary sat back on the seat and said in a shaky voice, "Melvin, I've enjoyed our time together, I really have. But deep down in my heart, I feel like we're not meant to be together."

She hardly had the courage to look up to meet his eyes; instead, she just stared at her lap as he guided his horse down the road, "I just feel like we're trying to force things…we're trying to make a romance work when it shouldn't be happening. It isn't coming easy."

"Mary," Melvin's voice sounded pleading as he explained, "I want things to work…I want…" Suddenly his voice trailed off, and he shook his head, "You know what? You're right. You're right, Mary. I have wanted things to be good between us, but they just aren't. You're a great girl, and I enjoy spending time together, but I know that I don't feel like a beau should."

Something about hearing him confirm her own feelings made Mary experience a mixture of sadness and relief.

As Melvin pulled into her parents' drive, he reached out and put a friendly arm around Mary's shoulder, "Thanks, Mary. Thank you for doing what is right."

Mary forced a smile and nodded her head, "Thank you for letting me."

Chapter Nine

Samuel took a deep breath as he stood awkwardly in Yoder's store, looking over their wide selection of merchandise. He'd drawn the names of Amish girls in the past during the holiday gift exchange and while shopping had been difficult, he had been happy to settle with any gift that he could find.

But Mary was different.

She might not like him, but Samuel wanted to at least give Mary a gift that meant something. He wanted to have the satisfaction of knowing that she had a gift that was worth keeping.

Glancing over the selection, Samuel let his eyes travel across an array of combs, brushes, and hair pins. No matter what he looked at, nothing seemed right for Mary.

"Well hello there, Samuel!" The familiar voice of Sarah rang out in his ears, warning Samuel that she was quickly approaching.

Turning around, Samuel smiled as the Amish girl walked up to his side, a smirk on her face. Samuel knew that he was forcing his smile…every time that he was around Sarah, he found himself forcing everything.

"What are you doing?" Sarah asked as she reached out and took Samuel's arm in her own, "Looking for a gift for someone special?"

Glancing back toward the items, Samuel shrugged and replied, "Shopping for the gift exchange."

Her arm felt uncomfortable on his, and he longed to push it away; however, he wasn't sure how to do that without hurting her feelings. Honestly, Samuel had never meant to lead Sarah on and yet, it seemed that while he did nothing to give her confidence in a relationship, she had just decided that he was her boyfriend.

"Do you want to exchange gifts with each other?" The question took Samuel totally by surprise. He was even more stunned when she scooted closer and leaned her head against his shoulder.

Samuel knew that the other Amish in the store were watching, obviously thinking that they were a couple.

It's time to put a stop to this! Samuel realized, his face growing warm.

Turning, he motioned Sarah toward the door as he explained, "I think that it's time we had a little talk."

Sarah smiled and nodded her head, following him outside. Taking her toward his buggy, Samuel motioned for her to get up on the seat.

"Let's take a little ride down the road," Samuel suggested.

As he climbed up on the buggy seat beside Sarah, Samuel found himself glancing at her every few minutes, trying to gauge what she was thinking. Her round face looked so carefree; she was obviously oblivious to all that he was about to tell her. It seemed that she truly believed that they were a happy couple. How could she not see that he was miserable?

"Sarah," Samuel started slowly as he edged his buggy farther away from the store, "I know that we've been spending a lot of time together here lately. You've been having me take you to and from the singings…and I haven't minded because I know that your brother and his girlfriend need their time alone."

Sarah smiled and nodded her head, "I haven't minded one bit either, Samuel! I've really enjoyed our time together."

Sucking in a deep breath, Samuel felt terrible as he forced himself to continue, "But, Sarah, things are starting to go a little bit overboard. When we go places…well, people are starting to think that we're courting! When you take my arm and lean your head against my shoulder…well, it just gives people the wrong impression!"

Shrugging innocently, Sarah's eyes got big and she asked, "And what's so wrong about them thinking we're courting?"

This was even harder than Samuel would have imagined. Shaking his head again, he slowed the horse to a stop and bluntly said, "Sarah, you are a nice person. You are a kind, good person…but you are not the girl for me. I appreciate that you want to spend time with me…."

Suddenly, Sarah's entire demeanor seemed to change. She sat up straight and jutted out her bottom jaw, her eyes narrowing as she exclaimed, "Are you…are you breaking up with me?"

Lifting the reigns along with his hands, Samuel tried to confirm her words kindly, "Sarah, I guess you could call it breaking up…but, honestly, we can't break up because we never were actually together!"

Sarah's face grew such a bright red color that Samuel thought she might explode. He had never seen her or anyone else look so angry before. She balled her hands up into fists and let out a huff before announcing, "Samuel Wittmer, I have never known a man who was so…so dirty! So sleazy! I can't believe that you led me on like this!"

Samuel opened his mouth to say something but before he had a chance to formulate words, Sarah started to climb down from the wagon.

"Sarah," Samuel started to sputter, "I don't mean to hurt your feelings…at least let me drive you back to the store…"

As her feet hit the ground, Sarah crossed her arms against her chest and looked at Samuel with hate-filled eyes. "Thank you very much, Mr. Wittmer, but I can walk. Good day!"

And with that, she was gone.

Samuel found himself sitting alone in his buggy. He was so relieved that the talk was over. He hated being alone but surely being single was much better than being with someone he didn't actually care for.

***

Mary didn't have the heart to tell her parents that she had broken things off with Melvin. She knew how disappointed they would be when they found out. Besides, while Mary knew that it was the right thing to do, there was a part of her that almost missed his attention.

When Sunday night came, Mary chose not to attend the young peoples' gathering. The idea of seeing both Melvin and Samuel seemed too difficult to bear. Instead, she sent her gift with a friend and decided to spend her Sunday evening visiting with her old friend, Willa.

"We sure are glad that you came tonight," Willa announced as Mary took a seat in a rocking chair by the stove, "Carl and I sure do enjoy the company when we have it!"

Smiling, Mary leaned back in her seat and took in a deep breath. It felt good to finally just sit down with friends and relax. She hoped that their time together would rid her mind of the painful thoughts that were floating through her head.

"It's a shame that you didn't get to go to the singing, though," Carl threw in as he stepped into the room and put another log on the fire.

Giving a shrug, Mary tried to explain, "I guess I'm not sorry. I wanted to skip it…needed some time away from…well, problems that I'm having."

Willa reached out and put a sympathetic hand on Mary's arm.

"Seems like everyone is having romantic troubles this time of year," Carl announced with a laugh as he sat down next to his wife, "Tis the season to be heartbroken!"

"What's that supposed to mean?" Willa asked with a roll of her eyes, his humor obviously lost on her in this situation.

Carl shrugged and explained, "Oh, I was talking to Samuel Wittmer the other day, and he was telling me about all kinds of woman problems that he's been having."

"Samuel?" Mary felt her interest immediately pique at the mention of his name. When had Samuel ever had woman problems? It seemed that he was an expert at cutting off those he didn't like and attracting those he did.

"Yeah," Carl said with a sad sigh, sobering as he considered the truth of his words, "He says that some girl is after him…a girl that he doesn't even like. She won't leave him alone while the girl he does like doesn't like him at all…" Suddenly, Carl's face went white and his eyes got large as he glanced at Mary. "Oh…I've said too much…I wasn't supposed to…I'm sorry, I wasn't thinking about who…"

Mary's mind suddenly started rushing in a million different directions. What did Carl mean?

Willa obviously wondered the same thing. She reached out and put a hand on her husband's shoulder, "Carl…what is this all about? What do you mean?" Glancing toward Mary, Willa was almost asking for permission as she said, "Carl, is this about Mary?"

Carl's face grew red as he admitted, "Well, I didn't mean to just butt my nose in…but it is about Mary. Samuel thought that she liked him…they even spent time together…when he realized that Mary didn't like him back, it really broke his heart!"

"When he realized I didn't like him?" Mary exclaimed, rising to her feet, overwhelmed with the ridiculousness of his statement. "What are you talking about? He's the one who doesn't like me!"

"No," Carl insisted, shaking his head. "He's pretty sure that you don't like him."

"Mary," Willa was the voice of reason that interrupted their disagreement, "What exactly happened between you and Samuel? How did things go from the two of you having a good time together to realizing that he supposedly didn't like you?"

Looking down at the floor, Mary tried to remember, "Well, we sat together and had a good time at the singing….I had backed into him and that's how we started talking. Then, when it was over, he offered to take me home…" Realization suddenly filled Mary's mind. Her mouth dropped open and her eyes got large as she exclaimed, "Oh, dear! I turned him down! I hadn't even realized…No wonder he hasn't approached me again! I was just trying to save him the trouble of taking me home…I didn't mean to hurt him!"

"You turned him down?" Willa repeated with a shake of her head, "Mary! How could you? Of course, he would think that you didn't like him after that!"

Mary wanted to explain, but she didn't have the time, "No time to talk any longer!" she exclaimed. "Carl, can I borrow your buggy? I've got to get to that singing!"

Chapter Ten

Samuel had dreaded the singing more than he had ever remembered dreading anything else. He hated the idea of seeing so many happy people when he was so miserable. The thought of seeing Sarah again was awful and trying to give Mary her gift was certain to be awkward.

When he reached the singing, Samuel had made himself so nervous that he could hardly force himself to go into the house. Instead, he stood in the barn by his buggy, trying to gather his courage.

The night air was getting chillier by the minute and as he looked out the open barn door, Samuel could see snowflakes falling freely down from the sky.

"Please, Lord," Samuel whispered under his breath, "Help me through this!"

Suddenly, a new buggy came into sight, its driver urging the horse along at top speed. Samuel narrowed his eyes, trying to make out who it might be.

Worrying that there might be some sort of trouble, Samuel hurried out of the barn to meet them.

As the driver pulled the buggy to a stop in the midst of the yard, Samuel could see that it was a young woman, alone, with the reigns clasped between her hands.

"Mary?" Samuel's voice almost shook as he recognized the driver and spoke her name aloud, "Mary, is that you? Are you alright?"

Mary practically jumped down from the buggy seat.

"Samuel," Mary announced, her voice sounding unusually firm, "I need to talk to you…and I need to talk right now." Sucking in a deep breath, she continued, "Several weeks ago, you and I sat together at one of these singings and we had a good time…at least, I had a good time. But somehow, everything changed. What changed?"

The entire conversation was taking Samuel by complete surprise. Shrugging, he tried to explain, "When I asked you to go home with me in my buggy, I thought you made it pretty obvious that you weren't interested. I felt so foolish…like I'd just been a bother to you. I don't want to be someone who just gets in the way or is obnoxious!"

Reaching out, Mary

uncharacteristically put her hands on his shoulders to stare him in the face, "Do you still like me?"

Samuel raised his eyebrows as he asked in return, "Do you like me?"

"Yes." Mary replied firmly, her voice softening along with her eyes as she repeated, "Yes. Yes, I do."

"And I like you, too." Samuel whispered, suddenly overtaken by emotion. Reaching out, he grabbed Mary and wrapped her up in a hug, pulling her against him. Surely this was too good to be true! How was it possible that the girl he had admired for so long truly cared about him?

Standing in the midst of the falling snow, Mary let Samuel hold her in his arms. Never could she have asked for things to be any better! Never in her wildest dreams could she have imagined that Samuel cared about her and wanted her in his life.

"Mary," Samuel whispered as he pulled back from her and reached into his pocket, "I have something for you."

Mary watched as he retrieved a small package that was wrapped in colorful red paper. Taking the package in her hands, she looked up at Samuel in surprise as he explained, "I got your name in the gift exchange."

Turning the package over in her hands, Mary un-wrapped it slowly, observing the way that he had wrapped it with such tender care.

"Samuel," she breathed as she pulled off the paper and found herself staring at a tiny, hand-carved replica of the nativity scene,

"This is beautiful."

Although it was small enough to hold in her hand, the tiny manger had been carefully carved with precision, each curve done with excellence.

"I've never seen anything like it!" Mary exclaimed, her eyes continuing to study the piece.

"And you never will again," Samuel laughed as he sheepishly stuck his hands down in his black pants, "I made it…carved it myself. I wanted…well, I wanted you to have something nice."

Mary felt tears start to collect in her eyes as she looked at the gift that had been given to her.

"A nativity…" Mary whispered, "A reminder of the Lord's gifts to us." Looking up to meet the gaze of Samuel, she continued, "The Lord has given us so many things…and I now realize that your friendship is one of my greatest blessings."

Samuel reached out and took Mary back into his arms, holding her tightly against his black coat.

In the distance, Samuel and Mary could hear Sarah's obnoxious voice as she stepped out onto the back porch. Obviously, she was not alone since she was talking to someone.

"I absolutely love these hair clips you bought me, Melvin!" Sarah was gushing, "They're beautiful. Thank you so much!"

Mary strained to listen to her ex-boyfriend's reply as Melvin announced, "Not nearly as beautiful as you. Sarah, would you be willing to ride home with me in my buggy tonight?"

"I'd be delighted!" Sarah assured him, "Now, let's get back inside and join in on the singing!"

With that, their voices faded out of hearing distance. Melvin and Sarah? They were together now? It seemed so perfect1

Looking up into Samuel's face, Mary's eyes met his, and they both began to chuckle.

"Looks like it's been a good night for a lot of people," Samuel replied with a smirk. Sobering, he asked, "How would you like to go home in my buggy tonight? Or would you rather walk?" he added teasingly.

Mary smirked and shook her head, "I never want to walk again. I never want to go anywhere unless you're by my side. While I'll need to take Carl's buggy back to his house, I am more than happy to ride home with you from that point."

Leaning her head against his chest, Mary soaked in the beating of Samuel's heart as he continued, "Mary, I know that we've only known each other a little while, but I want you in my life. I want to court you."

His words made Mary's heart skip a beat. Looking up at him, she felt like her ears were surely deceiving her, "Samuel, are you sure?"

He nodded his head, "*Jah*. I want to go talk to your father about it…right now!"

This announcement made Mary almost frightened. She knew how much her parents had wanted her to be with Melvin, and she also realized that she had yet to tell them that she had broken off the budding relationship. But she wasn't going to turn Samuel down again.

"Okay," she whispered softly, "Let's get started that way."

But under her breath, Mary found herself softly whispering prayers for yet another miracle.

Chapter Eleven

When Samuel and Mary reached her parents' house, there were still lanterns burning brightly through the windows, alerting her that her family was still awake.

"Samuel," Mary grabbed a hold of his sleeve before he could get down from the buggy seat, "Samuel, I need to warn you that my parents…well, they may not like this. You see…they had their hearts set on me marrying Melvin."

Samuel nodded his head slowly, obviously trying to take in this new information. For a moment, Mary was afraid that he might be ready to back out on talking to them entirely, but then he announced,

"Well, I guess it's time to see how this goes then."

Taking a deep breath, she followed Samuel into the house and then led him to the sitting room where her mom, dad, Joan, and Joan's husband were gathered around the fireplace, chatting and making popcorn on the fire.

"*Daed, Mamm*," Mary struggled to find her voice as she motioned toward Samuel, "I'm afraid that I have a lot of explaining to do."

Her daed looked up from his bowl of popcorn in surprise, his eyes getting large as he announced, "That's not Melvin!"

Looking down at the floor, Mary admitted, "No, it's not. Melvin is going home with someone else tonight. I called things off with Melvin over a week ago. He was a good man, *Daed*," she hurried to admit, "But not the man for me." Reaching out and taking Samuel's hand in her own, she confessed, "This…this is the man for me. Samuel Wittmer."

Joan's mouth had dropped open, and her mother's eyes were as large as saucers. For a few moments, it seemed that no one was going to say or do anything; instead, it appeared that they were frozen in place. Finally, Mr. King reached down into his bowl of popcorn and took out a handful as he asked, "So, do you love this man, Mary?"

Mary nodded her head almost too fast as she hurried to assure him, "Yes, yes, I do, *Daed*."

"And I love her," Samuel was quick to add, "I haven't spent much time with Mary at this point, but I am eager to get to know her. I want to court her, and I want to be her steady boyfriend."

Mr. King shrugged and replied, "Well then, that's fine with me."

Mary felt her own jaw drop open as she stared at her father and then looked at her mother. Mrs. King was beginning to smile and even Joan and her husband were giggling.

"What on earth?" Mary exclaimed, "I thought that you were set on me marrying Melvin!"

Frowning, Mr. King shook his head, "*Ach*, no, child! I want to see you happy…I want to see you married…that's all I want!"

"We could tell from the start that you weren't happy with Melvin," Mrs. King hurried to add, "It's good to see you happy…with someone you care about."

Mary felt like the weight of the world had been lifted off her shoulders. Turning to look at Samuel, she realized that he looked just as surprised and happy as she felt. Reaching out, he put an arm around her waist and drew her closer to his side.

"Thank you, sir!" Samuel exclaimed, his face practically beaming, "Thank you so much!"

"You're home early," Mr. King announced as he motioned toward some empty rocking chairs, "Sit down…sit and spend some time with the family."

"Yes," Mrs. King was quick to agree, "I'll go get another couple bowls so that you two can have popcorn. And Samuel, on Christmas Day we are having a large get together of family and close friends. You will be there, of course."

Samuel let out a laugh, "Of course!"

Sitting down in one of the wooden rocking chairs, Mary felt like her eyes were magnetized to Samuel. He was hers. Finally, hers.

And this year, she would not be alone over Christmas; instead, she would have the man that she loved at her side as she celebrated the special holiday with her family.

This truly was one of the greatest Christmas blessings she had ever experienced. And she had only experienced it because she was willing to let go of her fears and allow Gott to be in control. Rather than settling for what seemed safest to her, she had let the Lord lead her to this great turn of events.

"Thank you, Lord," she whispered softly as she soaked up every second of the night, "Thank you so much for Christmas blessings!"

The End

More Amish Romance

Amish Tears

Amish Rebellion

Amish Heartbreak

Amish Secrets

Amish Questions

Made in the USA
Coppell, TX
05 December 2019